PUFFIN BOOKS

THE WITCH THAT WASN'T

Rose is sure that the large, old house on the corner of her street is inhabited by a witch. That's why, when returning from a walk with her father, she tries to hurry him past it. Later, her father tells Rose a story about himself as a boy and about someone who absolutely terrified him. For years the young Connor was scared of Gerry, a mysterious man with a dog, but no friends. For no particular reason Connor was terrified of Gerry and added his name to his 'List of Fears'. Until one day when he was out on the bog, Connor found his life in danger and the only one who could help him was Gerry. When Connor was finally forced to speak to Gerry he began to wonder how he could have been so frightened of him after all.

A warm, humourous story that will appeal to everyone who has ever had fears of their own. It is not only the special story of Connor's childhood in Ireland, but the present-day story of his daughter Rose, who is spooked by an old woman living in a city street.

Carlo Gébler was born in Dublin in 1954. He is a writer and director of films as well as a novelist. He lives in Northern Ireland.

The Witch That Wasn't

CARLO GÉBLER

Illustrated by Valerie Littlewood

PUFFIN BOOKS

PUFFIN BOOKS

Published by the Penguin Group
Penguin Books Ltd, 27 Wrights Lane, London W8 5TZ, England
Penguin Books USA Inc., 375 Hudson Street, New York, New York 10014, USA
Penguin Books Australia Ltd, Ringwood, Victoria, Australia
Penguin Books Canada Ltd, 10 Alcorn Avenue, Toronto, Ontario, Canada M4V 3B2
Penguin Books (NZ) Ltd, 182–190 Wairau Road, Auckland 10, New Zealand

Penguin Books Ltd, Registered Offices: Harmondsworth, Middlesex, England

First published by Hamish Hamilton Ltd 1991
Published in Puffin Books 1993
1 3 5 7 9 10 8 6 4 2

Text copyright © Carlo Gébler, 1991
Illustrations copyright © Valerie Littlewood, 1991
All rights reserved

The moral right of the author has been asserted

Printed in England by Clays Ltd, St Ives plc
Filmset in Baskerville

To India-Rose, Jack and Finn

Chapter 1

THE TIME WAS Sunday afternoon, the place was London, the season was deepest winter. In Acacia Avenue, a street of low terraced houses, the fog crept silently along the road and the first signs of frost sparkled on the pavement.

The street lights came on with their dull yellow lights, and the next moment two people came round the corner. There was Rose, aged eight. She had brown eyes and blonde hair which her mother had knotted into a French plait.

1

Rose was wearing her best red woollen dress under her coat, as well as Wellington boots, a beret and blue mittens.

Rose's hand rested in Connor's. Her father was thirty-five. Rose thought this was old but she had no sense what these years really meant. Her mother said she was lucky not to know. Her mother said she would have plenty of time, later on, to find out what it was like to get old.

Connor was stringy. His hair was short and his ears stuck out. The two things about the way her father looked which Rose liked best were the way his teeth were even and met in the middle and the tiny black flecks in the blue of his eyes. Connor said they were bits of bog.

He said they were thrown in his face when he was a child in Ireland, one day when he was helping the men to cut the turf, and they had stuck there.

When she was younger Rose had believed this. Now she didn't any longer believe yet Connor persisted in saying it was so. He couldn't give up a story once he'd started it, which was as much a part of him as his sticking-out ears or his even teeth.

Rose and Connor were on their way home from the Common. They'd spent an hour there exploring after their lunch, for they were new to the area and hadn't really been there properly before. Of course their exploring hadn't really amounted to much more

than stamping around on the wet
grass and watching the footballers
chasing about on the muddy
playing fields, while the seagulls
wheeled and screeched in the grey
sky overhead.

"Did you like the outing?" Connor asked.

He always said outing instead of walk.

"Bit cold though, wasn't it?" said Connor, before Rose could answer.

He often answered his own questions. Sometimes she objected but today she didn't. She had something else on her mind.

It was the corner. Ever since they had moved to their house in Acacia Avenue, a couple of months earlier, the house on the corner had been a worry and it still was. She glanced sideways at it while taking care that she appeared to be staring straight ahead. One had to take precautions where this house was concerned.

It was bigger than the others in the terrace. It had a brick wall instead of a privet hedge. The windows were a dismal green and there were shutters behind them. When they were closed, like they were today, Rose imagined the house was a giant sleeping toad; when the shutters were open, the toad was awake and waiting.

And this afternoon they were open and that meant only one thing; Mrs Pritchard was in.

Rose saw the curtain in the bow window downstairs twitching and suddenly, there was Mrs Pritchard's face, hovering behind the glass in the gathering gloom. She had a broken nose and red veins in her cheeks, and wild white hair.

"Quick," Rose whispered, squeezing her father's hand but staring straight ahead.

From the distant Common came the faint roar of the crowd, "Whhhhheeeeeyyy".

"Someone must have scored a goal," said Connor, ignoring his daughter.

"Scarper," she hissed.

She started to run, pulling him after her.

"What's the hurry?"

Connor let himself go half-a-dozen steps and then he pulled Rose back.

"You don't want to let Mrs Pritchard see you," Rose began breathlessly. She would have pulled him further but he stood firm and wouldn't let her.

"Why not?"

"Ken in the newsagents said she's an odd bird. The greengrocer calls her a queer fish. I think she's a witch."

Connor watched the breath curling out of Rose's mouth.

"And her house is haunted," she concluded.

"How's that?"

"Every time I go past it makes me feel funny."

"It looks the same as any other house if you ask me. Bit bigger, that's all."

Rose shook her head very seriously. Her purse was in her pocket and she drew it out.

She undid the popper. Inside she had two one pound coins; a yellow tube ticket; a coloured pencil with

a candy-stripe design on it; a small
ring with a green stone which she
had got from a Christmas cracker
the year before; a *Snoopy* rubber; an
empty pistol cartridge she had just
found on the Common; a Polaroid
of her brother Red, no hair and a
squashed-up face, taken the day he
was born; an *Amazing Hulk* pencil
sharpener; a flattened out wrapper
from a *Lion Bar* with a World

Cruise competition entry on it; a *Swan Vestas* match with a red tip; two hair bands used to hold her pony tail in place; a set of paper clips made into a bracelet; and a notebook. The notebook was square and homemade; it comprised of several sheets of paper, doubled in two and stapled together.

She opened it out and by the

yellow light drifting down from the
street lamp, Connor was able to
make out the words written on the
page.

My
Book of
spels
agenst
the
Witch at
the end
of my
Street

"I always keep this about me,"
said Rose solemnly, "to protect me
from her."

Chapter 2

CONNOR TURNED THE key in the lock of their house and opened the door. Rose rushed in and her father followed.

As she heard the latch click behind Rose felt the wonderful warmth of the hall all round her. She went to the mirror on the wall. It was oval-shaped and freckled. She saw her red nose. She was reminded of Rudolph the reindeer from her favourite Christmas song. She thought, it must have been very cold out there for that to happen.

She sniffed. She always liked coming in and smelling their house and she

liked the smell here more than the one of the flat where they had lived before. The main smell here was the wax from the red hall tiles but it was mixed with other smells; clean laundry; her mother's scent; the green shaving stick her father used; candle wax; her brother Red's *Playdough*; *Mr Sheen* furniture polish; and all the nice foods which got cooked in the kitchen.

It was in the kitchen that she found her mother. She was standing at the worktop. She had her back to Rose when her daughter came in. Her mother was called Eve. Her hair was long and wavy. It reached to the middle of her back. Her mother wore a green emerald at the neck of her blouse and earrings made from pieces of green coloured glass. Rose had made them in school.

Her mother was cutting out scones from a piece of rolled-out pastry using an upside-down wine glass. There was a patch of flour on her cheek. Red, the toddler, was standing on a chair at the sink filling a saucepan with water.

"Wassing-up, Wose," he called over to his sister. "Wassing-up." It was one of the things he liked doing most.

Red was two-and-a-half. His hair was curly, his eyes were brown like Rose's and he had pink, round, baby cheeks. He looked innocent but he wasn't.

"I think I'll light a fire," Rose heard her father saying from the fireplace in the living room. The house was open-plan and she was able to just walk through to the next room without having to use a door. She saw her father take an old newspaper, twist the

sheets into lengths and lay them in the
grate. As she stood watching him, she
unbuttoned her coat and pulled it off.

"Did I ever tell you the story about
Gerry?"

"No," said Rose, and she sat down

on the sofa. On her face she wore her
I-want-to-hear look.

"Hang up your coat and I'll tell
you."

When Rose came back he was
pulling three firelighters from a box.
She smelt the paraffin smell they gave
off.

Connor laid them into the middle of
the paper and placed the kindling

sticks on top. His fingers were greasy from the firelighters and he wiped them on the newspaper.

He struck a match and lit the end of a paper twist. The flame caught, appeared to hesitate for a moment as if undecided what to do, and then started to lick along the paper. It touched the edge of one of the firelighters and, an instant later, the whole block was alight.

Rose was on the sofa, and as the flames jumped upwards, she was able to see the sooty back of the chimney light up.

Then she glanced at the window and looked through to the garden outside where it was almost dark and thought to herself, this feels good.

Chapter 3

"WHEN I WAS a child, I lived with my grandmother and grandfather in Ireland," said Connor.

"I know that," said Rose.

She had visited the house where her father grew up. As she stared into the fireplace she could see a picture of Ballyragget in the flames.

"I used to be a terrible one for making lists," continued Connor. "We used to go out through the back door to the yard, so I tacked up a list there of everything I thought we needed

23

when we went up there.

Stick
Pail for the calves' milk
Rope for the dog
Torch in case we go into the
curing shed

Grandfather's cigarettes and matches
Ball
Gun
Toffees

"When we left for church, we went out through the front door, of course,

lest anyone saw us. So I put up
another list on the back of that door, of
everything we needed for church.

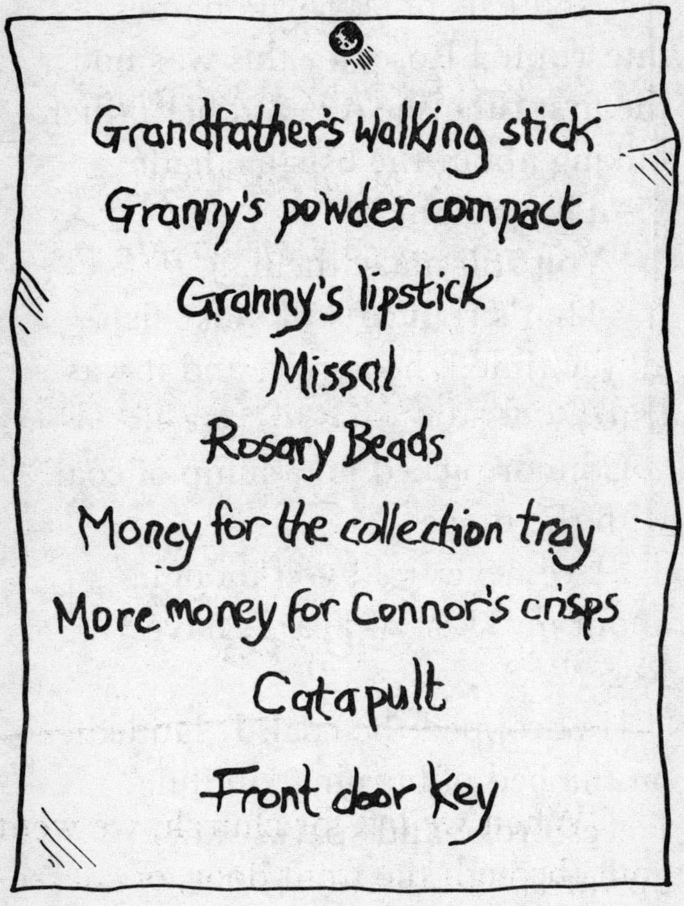

Grandfather's walking stick
Granny's powder compact
Granny's lipstick
Missal
Rosary Beads
Money for the collection tray
More money for Connor's crisps
Catapult
Front door key

"I used to make lists of favourite characters from stories and comics and lists of favourite smells and tastes . . ."

"And lists of favourite names," interrupted Rose, for this was not the first time she'd heard her father talking about the lists he made.

"That's right."

"You still make them."

"That's right. I still make lists all the time," he agreed and it was true.

Connor picked up a lump of coal with the tongs.

"I've never told you though about my 'List of Fears', have I Rose?"

He dropped the coal. It landed on the bed of burning kindling. Pieces broke and sparks shot upwards.

"My 'List of Fears' went like this:

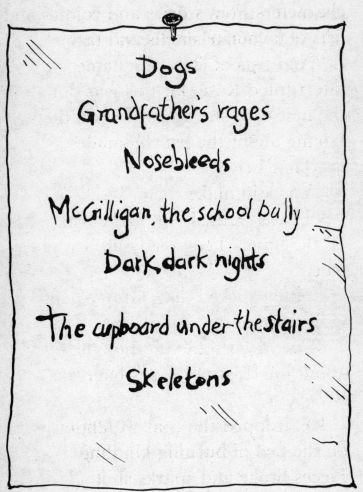

Dogs

Grandfather's rages

Nosebleeds

McGilligan, the school bully

Dark dark nights

The cupboard under the stairs

Skeletons

"Dark, dark nights," said Rose, savouring the words.

"And the darker, the worser," said Connor.

Chapter 4

"ONE WINTER'S AFTERNOON like this one, I was in the kitchen and it was all snug and warm from the big Aga which heated the house. I was reading *Treasure Island*. I was just at the part where Jim Hawkins tells about the Black Dog coming to his mother's pub, and the pirate showing his hand with its two missing fingers, like this."

Connor raised a hand with two fingers bent back.

"I was sitting at the table with the window beside me. I lifted my eyes from the book and looked out. I could

see the dwarf apple trees in the little
orchard shaking in the wind. I could
hear the copper beeches up by the yard
sighing and moaning. It was miserable
out there; set to storm and getting
dark. I was frightened of wind as well
as the night in those days. I liked being
in the light, being warm and keeping a
pane of glass between myself and a
winter's evening.

"'Connor,' I heard, 'Will you do me
a favour?'

"My granny came out of the larder,
holding one of her big jam jars filled
with blackcurrant jelly."

"No, Red!" cried Eve suddenly,
interrupting the story. "If any
more water gets on the floor, you'll
have to come away from the sink.
Look at the mess you're making!"

Rose looked across and into the

kitchen at Red on his chair, his
Paddington Bear apron tied
around his middle. He was staring
at his mother as if he didn't know
what she was talking about.

"Shush," Rose called over. "I
want to hear this story."

"So my grandmother said to me,"
continued Connor, 'Go down to the
hen run and close the door. It's getting
late. We don't want the fox to get in.'

"I didn't want to go. I was
comfortable and I wanted to read my
book and I didn't really like the look of
outside, as I told you. But in those
days, Rose, children had to do what
they were asked!

"I went out the back door, ran
across the flag and slipped through the
wicket gate onto the lawn. It wasn't a
lawn, of course, like we have here at

the back of this house. Our lawn at
Ballyragget was enormous. We grazed
the cattle on it.

"The sheds where the hens slept
were a hundred yards below the house.
I ran as fast as possible with my heart
beating. It wasn't pitch dark, just
getting dark, and I could make out the
shapes of the trees and the wall at the
bottom of the lawn running along the

side of the road. I could feel little drops of dew, which I kicked up, landing on my hands.

"I got to the shed and I was breathless. There were a few hens pecking at the huge tractor tyre, cut in half, which we used as a trough. I chased them through the little hole where they went in and out of the shed, and dropped the trap shut.

"Job done. I could go back to the Aga. I straightened up and was about to turn, when I saw him; a big figure with wild hair, walking towards me, whose whole face from his Adam's apple to his hairline, was covered by a purple birthmark.

"Just imagine. From chin to brow, like a dark plum, except for two shining eyes in the middle and a glinting row of white teeth underneath.

"His name was Gerry but he was
also called The Chancer. I'd seen him
before but never when I'd been on my
own. He'd always been around
Ballyragget but it was forgotten who
his parents were. He lived in a
broken-down old cottage three fields
away from us. He had no electricity;

his water came from a well; he slept in
a cardboard box on a bed of hay.

"He had no friends and his only
companion was the dog who was with
him. It was a mangy old thing with a
bit of Airedale and a lot of mongrel in
him. The dog's collar and lead were
made of old twine and there was more

of this around Gerry's waist, keeping his coat closed. He had lost all his buttons.

"At the front of Gerry's shoes, the uppers had come away from the soles and I remember the eerie, flapping noise which they made as he came towards me. Flip, flop, flip, flop . . .

"Gerry started to say something to me but I didn't wait to hear him finish. I turned round and started to run.

"I ran and ran. I felt as if I'd been stabbed very hard in the middle of my lungs. But I didn't give up or look back. I kept on running as fast as my legs would carry me, and I didn't stop until I was in through the back door.

"I threw myself into one of the kitchen chairs and dropped my head onto the oilcloth on the table. It felt cool and slippery. I was breathless and panting.

" 'What ever's the matter?' my granny asked, and when I got my breath back I told her I'd seen Gerry down by the hen run.

"She heard what I said without seeming in the least bit worried and then she said, 'Did he have something for me?'

"How did I know? I hadn't hung around to find out. Gerry terrified me.

39

" 'I don't know,' I said.

" 'He's probably got something for your grandfather,' continued my granny.

"Gerry was the poteen-maker. Do you know what that is, Rose?"

"Yes," replied Rose in a grown-up sort of way. Then she thought better of it and said, "Not exactly."

"It's a kind of whiskey. It's transparent, like water, rather than brown like ordinary whiskey. It used to be made all over when I was a youngster and the country people used to always have a bottle about their houses. They rubbed it on their chests for coughs and took it with hot water for a cold. They drank it for pleasure as well and, of course, it was illegal. The police were forever trying to catch

40

the ones who distilled it, like Gerry, and it was said he made the best poteen in our parish.

"Now I hadn't been back from the hen run more than a couple of minutes when I heard the spooky sound of Gerry's shoes.

"Flip, flop, flip, flop. I looked up from the kitchen table and there was his dark shape, lurching past the kitchen window.

"Flip, flop, flip, flop. I followed the sound of his footfalls as he made his way to our back door.

"Rat-tat-tat! I scuttled under the table and pulled the oilcloth down as far as it would go so that I couldn't be seen.

"I heard my granny scraping open the back door. There was the sound of a bottle being handed across to her

and there was a clink as she handed
money back to Gerry. I heard the two
of them talking in a low, hoarse
whisper and shivered.

"The door closed. I counted a
hundred slowly and finally came out
from under the table.

"'What were you doing under
there?' my granny asked.

"'Nothing,' I said.

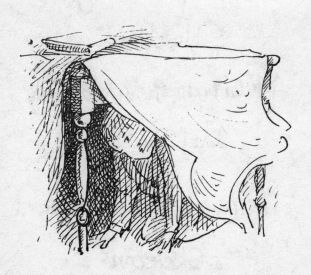

"I dug into my pocket and got out my 'List of Fears'. I got one of the pencils out of the *Fyson's Salts* tin by the wireless where all the pencils and pens in the house lived. I spread the paper out on the oilcloth.

Dogs

Grandfather's rages

Nosebleeds

McGilligan, the school bully

Dark, dark nights

The cupboard under the stairs

Skeletons

"I had a new item to add to the list and carefully I wrote it at the bottom.

Gerry, the poteen-maker —

Chapter 5

"TIME PASSED; A whole winter, a whole spring and then it was summer . . .

"One afternoon, I went up to the bog. It was grandfather's bog. It was a big, damp, flat place, at the end of the valley. There was a lake with a single swan who glided up and down all day long.

"All over the bog there were deep trenches where the turf had been cut. The turf was piled in mounds to dry. We used to burn it in the fires at home.

"I wandered along. I had an ash stick which I pretended was a sword.

46

Bog cotton grew everywhere and the plants waved in the wind. There were big clouds piled up like meringue in the sky.

"Presently I came to a huge trench, bigger than the one where we'd cut our turf earlier that summer, bigger than any I'd ever seen.

"I lay down on the ground and looked over the edge. I could feel the grass on my legs. In those days we wore short trousers.

"The sides of the trench were the colour of dark bitter chocolate. The rainwater lying in the bottom was black. I saw my reflection on the surface and the clouds behind. I spat several times and watched the ripples rolling outwards. Then I remembered the promise I had made to my granny.

"She knew she couldn't keep me out of the place so this was the agreement we had made. I was *never* to stray from the path and I was *never* to go near any of the trenches or the bog holes.

"If I fell in I would drown, she told me, even though I could swim. 'You see,' she said, 'once you fall in you can

never get out. The sides are soft and you can't get a grip on them. Unless someone comes and pulls you out, you'd drown in the end,' she said.

"One of our dogs that summer had fallen into a bog hole and it was just as she had told me. Rover thrashed in the water but couldn't clamber out. Grandfather lassoed him with a rope and that's how we got him back to dry ground.

"If I fall in, I thought, I'll never get out.

"I left the trench and returned to the path. I lashed with my ash stick at the long rushes I passed, at clods of turf which had fallen onto the ground and at the bog cotton which grew out of the dry brown earth.

"Suddenly, in the distance, I saw something which looked interesting. It was an old shed made from bits of corrugated iron. There was a chimney stack at the back. Clouds of blue-black smoke were rising from the end and drifting into the sky.

"I ran forward. I'd never seen this before on our bog. I went to investigate.

"Then I heard ferocious barking. There was a dog, over on my right-hand side, belting towards me.

"The next thing a figure loomed up

from behind the corrugated shed. I would have known the plum face with the shining eyes and the dirty coat tied with string around the middle to keep it closed, I would have known them anywhere.

"It was Gerry and I'd stumbled on his still, where he made his whiskey.

"He started to come towards me. He was speaking but I couldn't make out what he was saying.

"I stared and saw his horrible dog racing closer and closer.

"They're coming at me from both sides, I thought.

"I turned and started to run. I was in a complete panic. I saw the great flat bog stretching ahead of me and the sky, like a lid, closing down on top of it. Far away I could see the alder trees which marked the start of the Bog Road. I thought, if I can get to them, I'll be safe. If I can only get to those trees . . .

"At the same time I thought, I'll never get to them.

"The muscles in my legs were

quivering and felt weak and watery. I was gasping for breath and the pain I'd had the last time I'd fled Gerry, the hot, stabbing feeling behind the bone in the middle of my chest, I was feeling it again only ten times worse this time.

"I didn't stop, though. I kept running and I kept thinking, if I can just get to those trees, if I can just make it . . .

"Suddenly the clouds seemed to be swirling around me and my feet weren't on the ground any more. I looked down. I saw there was space underneath them. Because I had been looking ahead rather than where I was putting my feet, I had run straight off the edge of the huge trench. There was a ten foot drop and then . . .

"Smack! I hit the water. It was black and freezing. I gasped for my breath.

"A moment later I was under and looking up. The surface just over my head was silvery and behind were the swollen clouds and the hot summer sky.

"Everything was happening very fast but at the same time, everything was also going very slowly. That's the odd thing about a crisis.

"I'm going to drown, I thought. I remembered very clearly my granny saying the trenches and the bog holes were bottomless. I was going to sink down and down, for ever and ever, and no one was ever going to find me. No one was ever going to see me again.

"So there I was in the water, splashing, thrashing and sinking. I was so frightened I couldn't even swim properly. That was when I saw the

face of Gerry. He had jumped from the top of the trench and was at the water's edge. I saw his big, purple-coloured face and his wild hair. His dog was there beside him.

"He reached towards me. He's going to hold me under, I thought, he's come to drown me. My heart gave an enormous lurch and everything went black . . .

"Later, when I came to, I found myself in a twine seat. I was sitting by a hearth filled with glowing turf embers and bits of burning rubbish. There was a flat blackened tin of *Batchelors* peas, some sizzling lengths of bacon rind and a piece of the greaseproof paper which the local creamery butter came wrapped in."

"Where were you?" asked Rose.

Connor raised a finger. It was

his "All-in-good-time" signal. She knew it well.

"I looked up from the fire and round the room in which I found myself.

"There was a thatch roof above me, the yellow rushes black with smoke.

The floor was bare earth, hard and uneven. There was a single, tiny window with green mould growing on the inside of the glass. A wallpapering table with dozens of bottles on it stood against the wall. Straw was piled in a box in the corner. There was a filthy pillow on it; this was obviously the bed. A picture of Jesus, torn from a magazine, was tacked up by the door.

"But where was this?" repeated Rose.

"At my feet lay a dog. He was sleeping quietly, his chest rising up and down, up and down . . .

"Where am I? I thought, Where am I? I heard a voice going, 'Tra la la la la la la,' and through the open door do you know who walked in?

Rose shook her head.

"Gerry, with his great purple face,

the shining eyes and the glinting teeth.
I was in his cottage, wrapped in his
blanket. I was sitting by his fire. His
dog was on the floor beside me."

"No! Red, no!" came the sound
of Rose's mother suddenly. There
was a splash and a peal of laughter.

Rose and Connor turned to look towards the kitchen.

Eve came out. She was holding Red, swathed in a towel.

"He filled the sink with water," she explained, "and then he managed to fall in."

She carried Red over to the fire, took off the wet clothes and began to towel him dry.

"Red is like you falling into the trench in the bog," said Rose to her father.

"I suppose he is."

Eve said, "So you're telling her that story."

"He is," said Rose. "Now shush, until we hear the end. And I don't want to hear you making any noise either, Red, otherwise you'll have to go up to your bedroom."

"Red went swim," said Red with great delight.

"Now you be quiet," repeated Rose.

Sometimes, Rose could be a bit bossy.

Chapter 6

"GERRY WAS CARRYING an old box filled with turf when he came in. He walked over and started to throw the pieces onto the fire.

" 'You fell in,' he said over his shoulder, 'but we fished you out, myself and the dog.'

"I was absolutely terrified. But then I thought, why's he turned his back on me to stoke the fire. He wouldn't do that if he meant to do me harm, would he? Nor would he have left the door open, either. It's funny, you can be worried as anything and at the same time, you can have these calm, cool thoughts.

"Gerry picked a blackened kettle off the floor and tipped it to see if it was full. A great dollop of water splashed into the fire. There was a loud hiss and a cloud of steam rose up.

" 'You could have drowned up there on the bog,' he said. 'Not a good place up there, for a boy. You may get into a bog hole but you never get out, you know.'

I could smell the stale smell of sweat from his clothes. I had never been this close to him.

" 'Sometimes, cutting turf,' he said, 'they find ones up there who drowned two hundred years ago.'

"He hung the kettle on a crane hook and swung it over the flames.

" 'But they won't be finding you,' he

said, 'will they?' He started to chuckle.
After a moment or two I laughed with
him. That was when I knew everything
was going to be all right.

"When the kettle boiled, Gerry
brewed up some tea in an old brown
teapot with a chipped spout.

"'I don't have any milk,' he said.
'No cows here like you have above at
home.'

"He brandished a tin of *Nestlé's*
Condensed Milk.

" 'This is better though,' he said.

"He got a hammer and nail and made two holes in the lid. He tipped the tin over the first cup. The liquid came out in a thin jet and was yellow.

"He gave me the first cup and I took a sip. The tea was very strong and very sweet.

"We started to talk. I don't remember what we talked about but I

do remember thinking after a while, he isn't frightening at all.

"And quite soon I stopped noticing his face was purple all over.

"The dog was nice too, I discovered. I gave him the end of my tea to drink out of the saucer and he lapped it up. His name was Spot.

"By asking questions I was able to put together what had happened up on the bog.

"When he heard the dog, Gerry came out to see who it was. If I'd been the police, he told me, he'd have had to make a run for it.

"That was when I saw him. At the same time I saw the dog and panicked. By this stage, he had realised who I was and was waving and shouting out, 'It's all right. The dog won't bite. You're safe.'

"But I was too alarmed to hear. I turned and ran and that was when I went over the edge of the trench. He ran round the side of the trench and got down from the path to where I was. The rest I knew.

"I finished the tea and Gerry walked me home. My shoes squelched and he sang. As I opened the back door of Ballyragget he vanished and I was left standing on the steps in the blanket he'd lent me.

"I told my granny what had happened. I couldn't have avoided telling her even if I'd wanted to. Under the blanket I was still damp all over. She was angry at first and then she hugged me and made me swear never to go up to the bog again without a grown-up.

"She got down some dry clothes from the rack above the Aga.

"I went up to the bedroom to put them on. They were warm and felt good.

"When I came down again I found Granny had opened a tin of pineapple chunks. Tins of fruit were precious in those days. Granny kept her tins in the dining room, in a big old sideboard with a squeaking door. She called it her "safe". It could never be opened without her hearing. This was an old tin. It had been sent to her by some friend in London. It came from Fortnum & Mason's. It was so old there were dark spots on the label.

" 'For tea,' she said.

"The chunks were sweet and sharp at the same time and when we had finished she let me drain the thick, sweet juice from the tin.

" 'What's the celebration in aid of?' asked my grandfather. He was passing through the kitchen on his way to the breakfast room for a smoke.

" 'Connor got wet, poor thing.'

" 'Oh yes,' grunted my grandfather and passed on. I was grateful she hadn't gone into detail. He could get into terrible rages and the bald statement that I'd fallen into a trench in the bog, could well have set him off. She gave him the details later when he was in a good mood but I'm running ahead with my story.

"We finished tea. Granny went into the scullery to mix up the chicken meal with milk which she was going to feed the hens. I went over to my clothes which were drying on the rack above the Aga. I fished into the pocket of the trousers and pulled out a wet piece of paper.

"I opened it on the oilcloth and a little puddle of brown bog water formed around it. It was my 'List of Fears'. Can you remember what they were, Rose?"

Rose said, "Oh yes."

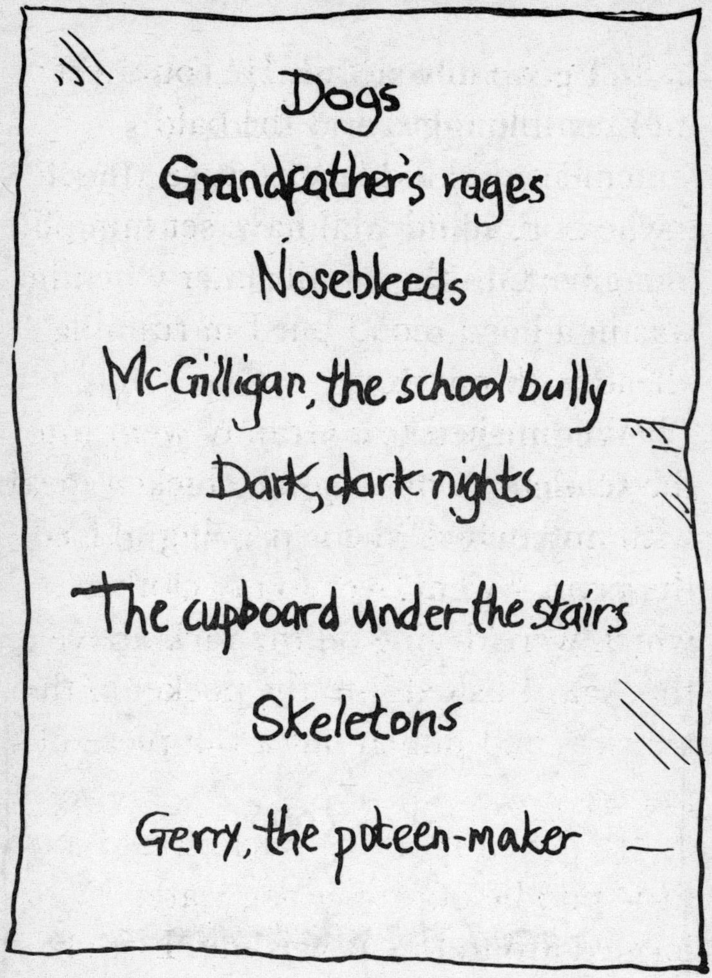

Dogs

Grandfather's rages

Nosebleeds

McGilligan, the school bully

Dark, dark nights

The cupboard under the stairs

Skeletons

Gerry, the poteen-maker

Connor nodded. "Very good."
"Were you still frightened of
dogs?" she asked.

73

"I probably still was," he said. "Even though Gerry's dog was nice, I was still wary of them. But I wasn't thinking about dogs at that moment. I was thinking of something else."

"You were thinking Gerry didn't belong there anymore?"

Connor nodded again.

"So you took your pencil and crossed it out."

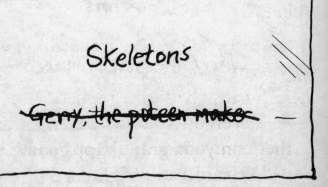

Chapter 7

"I WENT INTO the village the next day with my granny. She'd told Grandfather what had really happened when I'd gone to bed and he'd gone in that night and told everyone the story. I think he'd had a good few drinks out of it.

" 'So you nearly drowned,' people passing us called out.

" 'I nearly did,' I replied.

" 'Weren't you lucky Gerry was up there on your grandpappy's bog,' people said.

" 'Yes, I was,' I agreed.

75

"Everyone was winking all the time. It amused them, you understand, that I should have stumbled on Gerry's still in an afternoon, when the police had been trying to catch him for years and got nowhere."

Rose nodded. She found all this winking a mystery as well but she didn't ask about it. She could tell the story was coming to an end and what she wanted more than anything was to keep it going.

"What happened then?"

"Well, now came the good bit," said Connor.

"Mr Hickey came out of his shop and gave me a threepenny bit for my troubles and Mrs Mullen in the chemist's gave me a sixpence. Soon I had money collected from all over the village.

I bought myself a *Beano* and a *Dandy*.

"We walked home then, Granny and I. Past the creamery, past the new school, past the old workhouse.

"We came to the avenue up to our house a mile out of the village. There were chestnut trees growing around the gate. The leaves were green in the sunshine and I could see the hard green shapes of the conkers forming, although it would be months before they'd fall.

"Beside our gateway was a lane. It was completely overgrown with brambles and gorse bushes. No car or cart ever went up there. The path in the middle was just wide enough for a man, or a boy. At the end was Gerry's cottage.

"'I think I'll just call up to see him,' I said.

" 'Be sure and be home for your dinner at one,' said Granny, 'and don't be late.'

"I gave her the comics to take up to the house for me, and disappeared into the green tunnel that led up to Gerry's place."

Chapter 8

"WHAT HAPPENED THEN?" asked Rose.

"Oh, I can't remember," said her father. "He may not even have been home that morning. He may have been out on the bog and I couldn't go up there to see him, could I?"

"No, you'd promised your granny, and a promise is a promise is a promise."

"Oh no," sighed Eve and everyone turned to see what the matter was.

81

While they had all been listening, Red had put a piece of coal in his mouth, decided he didn't like the taste, and then found it was much more fun to rub

coal dust all over his face and chest.

"I don't know what to do with this child," said Eve. "He's dropped a bag of flour all over the floor; he's flooded the kitchen; he's fallen in the sink; and now he's painted himself with coal."

"He looks like Gerry, doesn't he?" said Rose.

"Scones smell good," said her father. "How long until they're ready?"

"Ten minutes."

"Tell you what Rose, why don't we call on the witch, our witch I mean. I'm sure she won't be wearing a pointed hat or anything . . ."

They pulled their coats on. Outside it was a dark winter's evening.

"We can knock on her door and just introduce ourselves," said Rose.

"That's it," agreed Connor.

"We can say, we moved in a couple of months ago and we thought it was time we introduced ourselves."

"Okey-dokey."

She put her hand into her father's pocket and found his hand.

"Dad?"

"Yes."

"You know when you were living with your granny?"

"Yes."

"What happened under the stairs?"

"My darling Rose," he said, "that is another story."

The Village Dinosaur

Phyllis Arkle

"What's going on?"
"Something exciting!"
"Where?"
"Down at the old quarry."

It isn't every small boy who finds a living dinosaur buried in a quarry, just as it isn't every dinosaur that discovers Roman remains and stops train smashes. Never have so many exciting and improbable things happened in one quiet village!

ADVENTURE ON SKULL ISLAND

Tony Bradman

Life for a pirate family is one long adventure!

When Jim finds a treasure map of Skull Island on board the *Saucy Sally*, he knows he and his sister Molly are in for an exciting time. But little do they know that their great enemy, Captain Swagg, is after the same treasure – and is determined to get there first!